Groundwood Books / House of Anansi Press
110 Spadina Avenue, Suite 801, Toronto, ON M5V 2K4

Distributed in the USA by Publishers Group West
1700 Fourth Street, Berkeley, CA 94710

We acknowledge for their financial support of our publishing
program the Canada Council for the Arts, the Government of Canada
through the Book Publishing Industry Development Program (BPIDP)
and the Ontario Arts Council.

ONTARIO ARTS COUNCIL
CONSEIL DES ARTS DE L'ONTARIO

Library and Archives Canada Cataloguing in Publication
Demers, Dominique.
[Tous les soirs du monde. English]
Every single night / Dominique Demers, Nicolas Debon.
Translation of: Tous les soirs du monde.
ISBN-13: 978-0-88899-699-2
ISBN-10: 0-88899-699-3

I. Debon, Nicolas II. Title. III. Title: Tous les soirs du monde. English.
PS8557.E4683T6813 2006   jC843'.54   C2005-905291-0
Printed and bound in China by Everbest Printing Co. Ltd.

Simon's dad smiles.
His son is right.
Now it's time for him to go to bed, too.

Every single night.
It's always the same, all around
the world...
It's time to go to sleep.

"That's all done, kid,"
whispers Simon's dad.
"There's nothing to be afraid of now."

Simon lies still.
He has fallen asleep.

Elves leap between continents and fairies shake loose their golden hair over the seas. Monsters and dragons and the creatures that haunt the night have gone into hiding. Magicians scatter dust from the stars and shake out powders from the northern lights. Now everything is under their spell. As long as the fairies are keeping watch, nothing bad can happen.

So Simon's dad
pulls up the covers,
all the way up this time.
With his hands resting gently
on Simon's head,
he says the magic words that
put the world of wonder
to sleep.

Simon sees…

Simon's dad smiles.

His son is right.
There is still one very
important place left.

"That's all done, kid,"
says Simon's dad.
"The whole sky is fast asleep.
You can go to sleep now, too."

Simon sighs and closes his eyes.
His dad gets up to leave.

But at the last minute,
Simon cries,
"No! You haven't finished!"

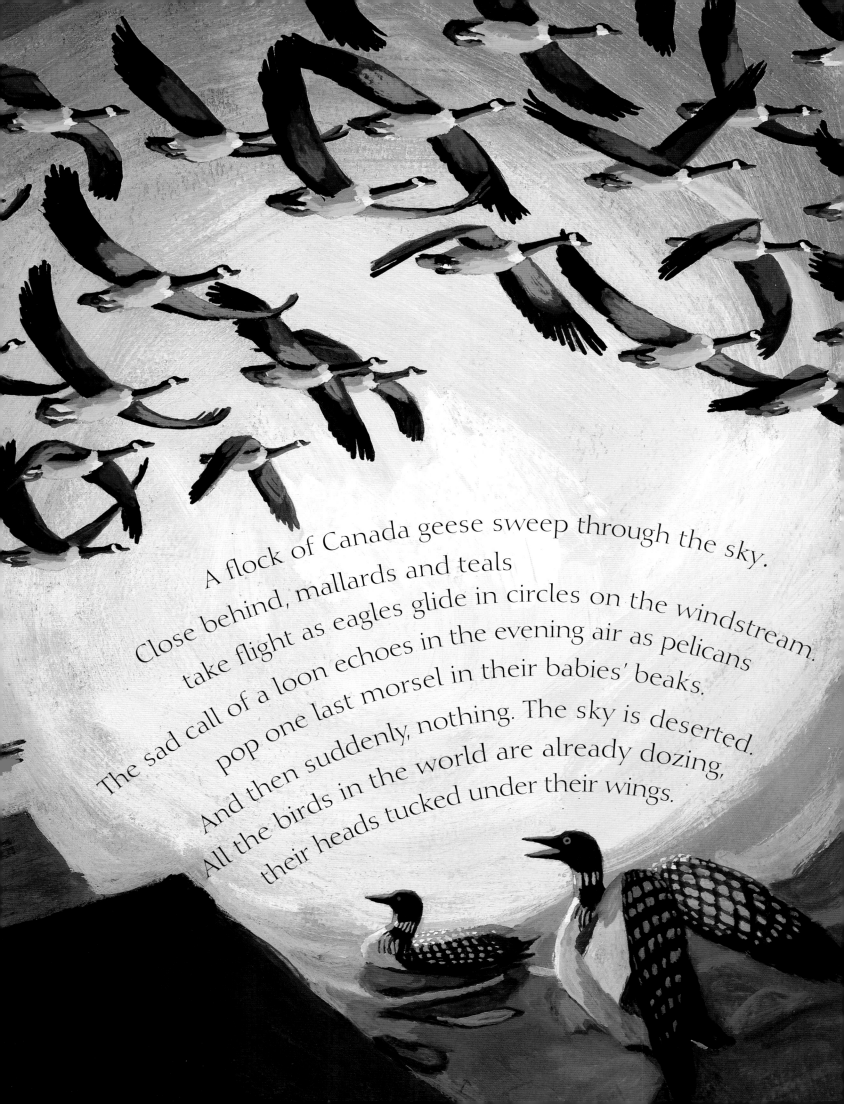

A flock of Canada geese sweep through the sky.
Close behind, mallards and teals
take flight as eagles glide in circles on the windstream.
The sad call of a loon echoes in the evening air as pelicans
pop one last morsel in their babies' beaks.
And then suddenly, nothing. The sky is deserted.
All the birds in the world are already dozing,
their heads tucked under their wings.

So Simon's dad pulls up the covers
just a little bit higher.
With his hands resting gently on Simon's
shoulders,
he says the magic words that put the sky to sleep.
He begins somewhere in the Americas.

Simon sees…

"That's all done, kid,"
says Simon's dad.
"The Arctic is fast asleep."

Simon stretches out,
and waits.

A herd of caribou lift their antlers.
A pack of white wolves prick up their ears.
Seals sniff the frozen air one last time
as bears gather their little ones
and head for their cozy dens.
The gentle veil of night settles over
the land of the midnight sun.

So Simon's dad pulls up the covers
just a little bit higher.
With his hands resting gently on
Simon's tummy,
he says the magic words that put
the white snow deserts, the icy tundra
and all the other cold lands to sleep.
He begins with Ellesmere Island
because the name is so pretty.

Simon sees…

"That's all done, kid,"
says Simon's dad.
"The oceans are fast asleep."

Simon blinks his eyes,
and waits.

Whales dive gracefully
through the great billowing waves.
Then sea horses, flying fish, dolphins, moonfish,
giant turtles and jellyfish join in one last
water ballet, an ode to the stars,
before gliding away into the depths of the sea.

So Simon's dad pulls up the covers
a bit higher.
With his hands resting gently
on Simon's knees,
he says the magic words that put the
oceans to sleep.
He begins with the Caribbean Sea.

Simon sees…

"That's all done, kid,"
says Simon's dad.
"Africa is fast asleep."

Simon yawns a little,
and waits.

Mighty lions shake their manes,
and roar so loud
that baobab trees quiver.
Then from every corner of the bush,
elephants, zebras, rhinoceroses,
giraffes, gazelles and cheetahs
race away under the moon.
They dash home to their dens, their lairs, their hideaways.
They run off to curl up in the arms of the night.

Simon's dad
begins with Africa.
He pulls up the covers just a little.
With his hands resting gently
on Simon's feet,
he says the magic words that
put the plains and the jungles to sleep.

Simon sees…

Every single night,
Simon's dad comes upstairs.
Now he is ready to put the world to sleep.
If he doesn't, Simon won't close his eyes.

Then, and only then,
Simon shouts out,

"Daaaaddd!!!"
"Daaaaddd!!!"

It's always the same,
every single night.

Simon sets about getting his
bed ready.
So he fluffs up his pillow
and folds back the blankets
before he climbs in, carefully.

Bedtime.

Simon yawns.
He puts on his pajamas, brushes his hair
and drinks a big glass of milk.
After he washes up from head to toe
and carefully brushes his teeth,
he climbs up the stairs.

Dominique Demers
& Nicolas Debon

Every
Single
Night

GROUNDWOOD BOOKS
HOUSE OF ANANSI PRESS
TORONTO   BERKELEY

Every

Single

Night

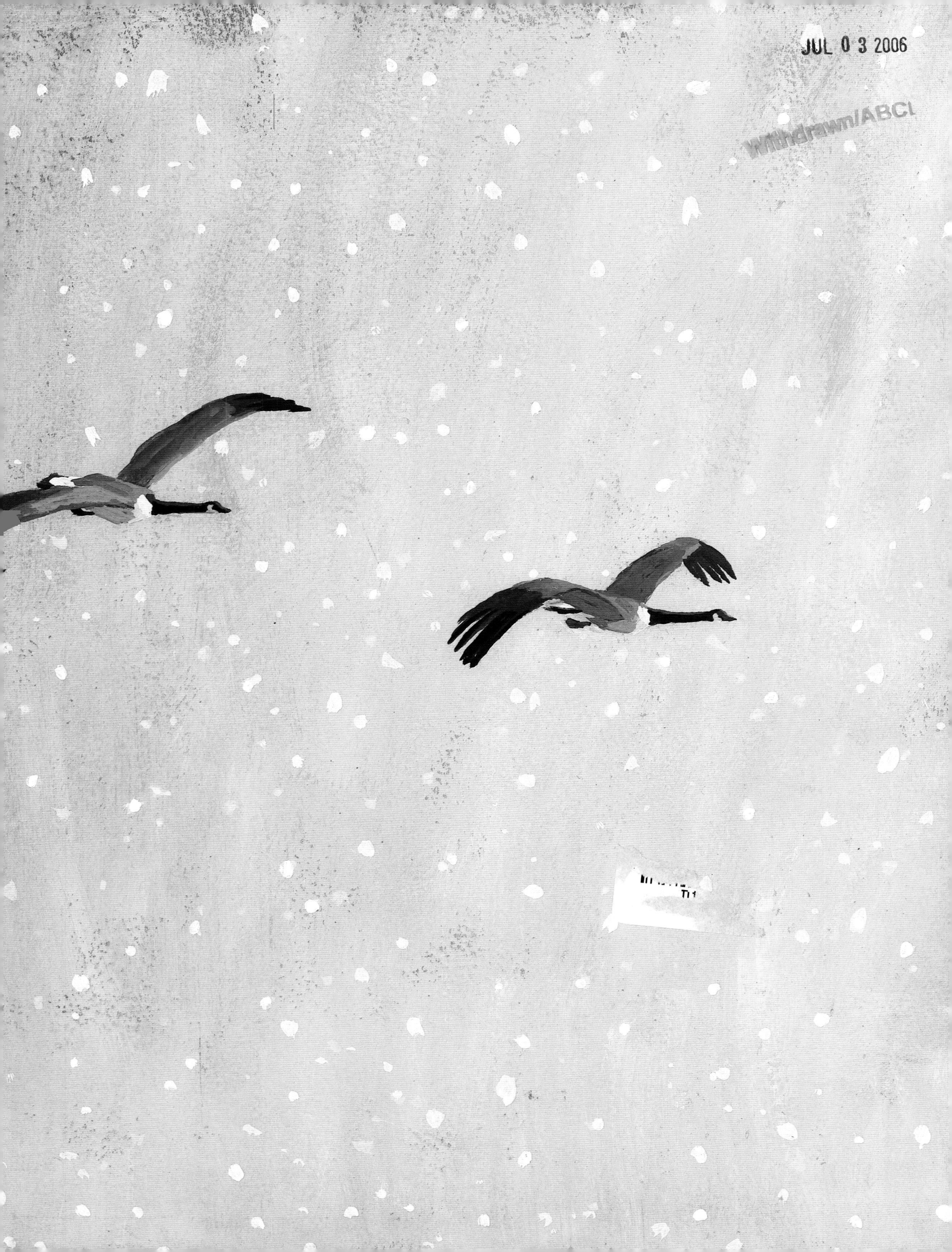